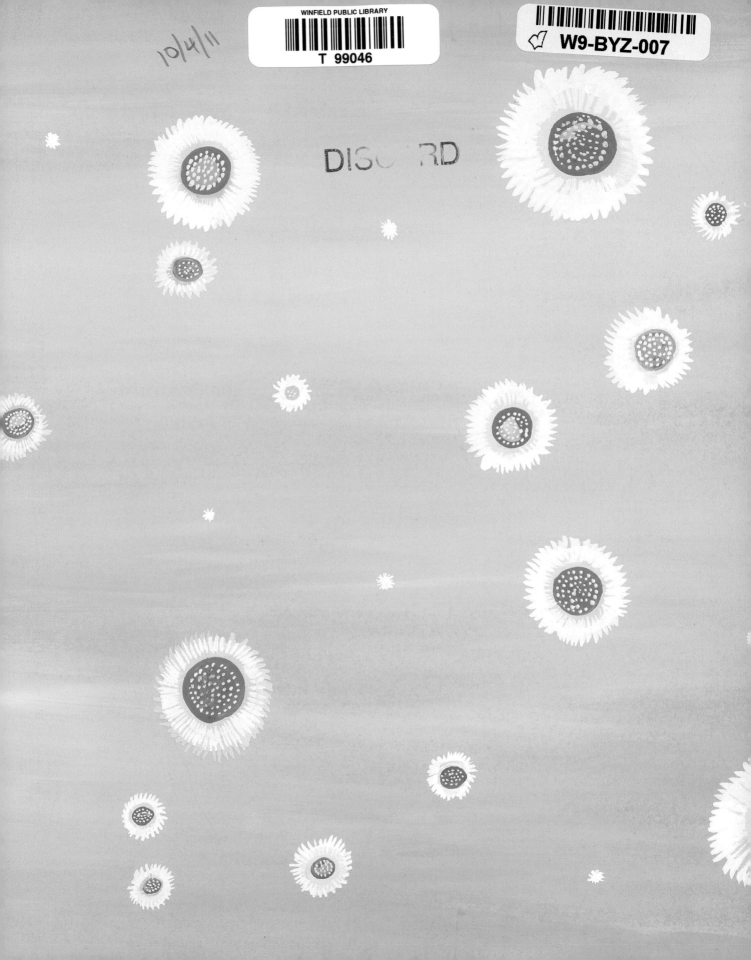

To Beth Terrill and David G.
Thank you, thank you.
—P.G.

For Pia and Isabel
—G.P.

Text copyright © 2011 by Phillis Gershator
Jacket art and interior illustrations copyright © 2011 by Giselle Potter

All rights reserved. Published in the United States by Random House Children's Books, a division of
Random House, Inc., New York.

Random House and the colophon are registered trademarks of Random House, Inc.

Visit us on the Web! www.randomhouse.com/kids

Educators and librarians, for a variety of teaching tools, visit us at www.randomhouse.com/teachers

Library of Congress Cataloging-in-Publication Data
Gershator, Phillis.
Moo, moo, brown cow, have you any milk? / by Phillis Gershator ; illustrated by Giselle Potter. — 1st ed.
p. cm.
Summary: Through rhyming text, farm animals are asked if they have items needed to prepare for a snack
and bedtime, such as wool for a blanket, down for a pillow, and milk to drink.
ISBN 978-0-375-86744-6 (trade) — ISBN 978-0-375-96744-3 (lib. bdg.)
[1. Stories in rhyme. 2. Domestic animals—Fiction. 3. Bedtime—Fiction.] I. Potter, Giselle, ill. II. Title.
PZ8.3.G3235Moo 2011
[E]—dc22
2010018767

MANUFACTURED IN CHINA
10 9 8 7 6 5 4 3 2 1
First Edition

Moo, Moo, Brown Cow,

Have You Any Milk?

By Phillis Gershator

Illustrated by Giselle Potter

RANDOM HOUSE 🏠 NEW YORK

Baa, baa,
black sheep,
have you any wool?

"Yes, sir, yes, sir, three bags full."

Does wool make a blanket for my bed?

"Yes, sir, yes, sir," the black sheep said.

Honk, honk, gray goose,
have you any down?

"Yes, sir, yes, sir,
half a pound."

Does down make a pillow for my head?

"Yes, sir, yes, sir," the gray goose said.

Cluck, cluck, red hen,
have you any eggs for me?

"Yes, sir, yes, sir, one, two, three."

Do eggs and flour make a loaf of bread?

"Yes, sir, yes, sir," the red hen said.

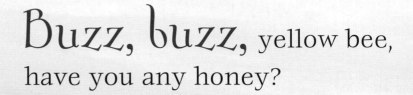

Buzz, buzz, yellow bee,
have you any honey?

"Yes, sir, yes, sir, sweet and sunny."

Does sun-sweet honey make a tasty spread?

"Yes, sir, yes, sir," the yellow bee said.

Moo, moo, brown cow,
have you any milk?

"Yes, sir, yes, sir, smooth as silk. "

Does milk make me sleepy before I go to bed?

"Yes, sir, yes, sir," the brown cow said.

"We're off to bed, too," the animals said,

"in the hive,

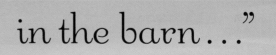

in the barn…"

"... in the coop,

in the shed."

green grass to chew . . ."

" . . . a golden grain of wheat or two,

Sleep tight, farm friends.
May I dream with you?

"Yes, sir, yes, sir, yes, please do."